WHERE'S COLUMBUS?

By
Anthony Tallarico

SMITHMARK

Copyright © 1992 Kidsbooks Inc. and Anthony Tallarico
7004 N. California Ave.
Chicago, IL 60645

ISBN: 0-8317-9284-1

This edition published in 1992 by SMITHMARK Publishers Inc.,
112 Madison Avenue, New York, NY 10016

SMITHMARK books are available for bulk purchase for sales promotion and premium use.
For details write or telephone the Manager of Special Sales, SMITHMARK Publishers Inc.,
112 Madison Avenue, New York, NY 10016. (212) 532-6600.
Manufactured in the United States of America

Christopher Columbus was born in Genoa, Italy in 1451.

FIND BABY CHRISTOPHER AS HE IS DELIVERED AND...

- ☐ Anchor
- ☐ Balcony
- ☐ Balloon
- ☐ Banana peel
- ☐ Banner
- ☐ Broken chair
- ☐ Broom
- ☐ Candle
- ☐ Cat
- ☐ Cow
- ☐ Dog
- ☐ Fish (2)
- ☐ Flowerpot
- ☐ Green bird
- ☐ Hearts (2)
- ☐ Horse
- ☐ Jester
- ☐ Kite
- ☐ Laundry
- ☐ Mermaid
- ☐ Mouse
- ☐ Oar
- ☐ Pillow
- ☐ Plate
- ☐ Propeller
- ☐ Rabbits (2)
- ☐ Rope
- ☐ Snake
- ☐ Soccer ball
- ☐ Telescope
- ☐ Top hat
- ☐ Trunk
- ☐ TV antenna

Did she do her homework? What's for sale?

Throughout Columbus's youth, many people believed that boats fell off the edge of the world and into the hungry mouths of sea creatures.

LOOK FOR YOUNG COLUMBUS AT THIS STORY-TELLING SCENE AND...

- ☐ Apple
- ☐ Arrow
- ☐ Ball
- ☐ Bow
- ☐ Candle
- ☐ Chef
- ☐ Chicken
- ☐ Crocodile
- ☐ Dogs (2)
- ☐ Earmuffs
- ☐ Feather
- ☐ Fish (3)
- ☐ Flat globe
- ☐ Flowerpot
- ☐ Flying bat
- ☐ Goggles
- ☐ Ice-cream cone
- ☐ Key
- ☐ Musician
- ☐ Paintbrush
- ☐ Periscope
- ☐ Pie
- ☐ Pot
- ☐ Propeller
- ☐ Roller skates
- ☐ Screwdriver
- ☐ Snowman
- ☐ Spoon
- ☐ Squirrel
- ☐ Sword
- ☐ Target
- ☐ Tears

Who is Uncle Zeke?
What is Alma doing?

Christopher Columbus was the oldest of five children.

SEARCH FOR COLUMBUS AS A TEEN AT HIS FATHER'S WORKPLACE AND...

- ☐ Bottle
- ☐ Carrot
- ☐ Clothespin
- ☐ Comb
- ☐ Crayon
- ☐ Fish
- ☐ Flower
- ☐ Football
- ☐ Grapes
- ☐ Hammer
- ☐ Hearts (4)
- ☐ Horse
- ☐ Hourglass
- ☐ Ice skate
- ☐ Keys (3)
- ☐ Mice (4)
- ☐ Moth
- ☐ Necktie
- ☐ Oilcan
- ☐ Pirate
- ☐ Ring
- ☐ Saw
- ☐ Scissors
- ☐ Sheep (2)
- ☐ Toothbrush
- ☐ Turtle
- ☐ Yo-yo

What is Christopher's father's occupation?
Who is late?

The explorer that Columbus admired most was Marco Polo.

HUNT FOR COLUMBUS AS HE DAYDREAMS ABOUT THIS FAMOUS ADVENTURER AND...

☐ Apple
☐ Arrow
☐ Baseball cap
☐ Bell
☐ Car
☐ Elephant
☐ Feather
☐ Fish
☐ Flower
☐ Ghost
☐ House
☐ Ice-cream cone
☐ Jack-in-the-box
☐ Jack-o´-lantern
☐ Kite
☐ Lion
☐ Mouse
☐ Net
☐ Owl
☐ Paintbrush
☐ Pear
☐ Rabbit
☐ Ship
☐ Skull
☐ Stars (5)
☐ Tepee
☐ Umbrella

How long was Marco's stay?
What's the emperor's name?
Why does Christopher have to go home?

Christopher arrived in Portugal after a ship he was on sank during an attack by the French.

WHERE'S COLUMBUS AMONG THESE SHIP-WRECKED SAILORS AND...

- ☐ Accordion
- ☐ Arrow
- ☐ Bathtub
- ☐ Beachball
- ☐ Birdbath
- ☐ Bone
- ☐ Books (4)
- ☐ Broom
- ☐ Crayon
- ☐ Cup
- ☐ Drums (2)
- ☐ Envelope
- ☐ Fire hydrants (2)
- ☐ Fishbowl
- ☐ Football
- ☐ Horseshoe
- ☐ Kite
- ☐ Octopus
- ☐ Paper airplane
- ☐ Pencils (2)
- ☐ Periscope
- ☐ Phonograph record
- ☐ Pie
- ☐ Pillow
- ☐ Pizza
- ☐ Pot
- ☐ Shark fins (3)
- ☐ Top hat
- ☐ Trash can
- ☐ Treasure chest
- ☐ Worm

What city will Columbus go to?
Where was the boat going?

Christopher Columbus wanted to find the shortest route to the Indies by sailing west, not east from Portugal.

FIND COLUMBUS ON THE TROLL'S TOLL LINE AND…

- ☐ Alligators (2)
- ☐ Apple
- ☐ Artist
- ☐ Banana peel
- ☐ Cow
- ☐ Duck
- ☐ Elephant
- ☐ Flying bat
- ☐ Frying pan
- ☐ Genie in a lamp
- ☐ Ice skates (5)
- ☐ Ice-cream cone
- ☐ Kangaroo
- ☐ Little Red Riding Hood
- ☐ Lost boot
- ☐ Pig
- ☐ Rabbit
- ☐ Red wagon
- ☐ Roller skates
- ☐ Sacks (5)
- ☐ Sailboat
- ☐ Santa Claus
- ☐ Schoolbags (2)
- ☐ Ship in a bottle
- ☐ Skateboard
- ☐ Skier
- ☐ Snowman
- ☐ Telescope
- ☐ Tin man
- ☐ Tollkeeper
- ☐ Traffic helicopter
- ☐ Turtles (2)
- ☐ Umbrella
- ☐ Visitors (3)
- ☐ Walking stick
- ☐ Watering can

Who collects the tolls?
What's for sale? (2)

Portugal's rulers would not fund Columbus's plan to sail to the Indies.

LOOK FOR COLUMBUS IN THE KING'S COURT AND...

☐ Axe
☐ Bears (2)
☐ Bowling ball
☐ Broom
☐ Cactus
☐ Camel
☐ Candles (2)
☐ Chef's hat
☐ Dog
☐ Fish (2)
☐ Football
☐ Frog
☐ Hockey stick
☐ Hot dog
☐ Ice skate
☐ Igloo
☐ Key
☐ Lion
☐ Medal
☐ Paintbrush
☐ Pen
☐ Pot
☐ Quarter moon
☐ Shopping bag
☐ Sneakers
☐ Spoon
☐ Star
☐ Straw hat
☐ Train
☐ Truck
☐ Turtle
☐ Yo-yo
☐ Zipper

How many jokes does the jester have?
Who was a prince?

Christopher Columbus appealed to Queen Isabella and King Ferdinand of Spain for the money to begin his journey. Eventually, the queen and the royal treasurer gave him the funds.

SEARCH FOR COLUMBUS IN SPAIN AND…

- ☐ Alien creature
- ☐ Anchor
- ☐ Baseball
- ☐ Candles (3)
- ☐ Count Dracula
- ☐ Crowns (4)
- ☐ Cups (2)
- ☐ Dart
- ☐ Dog
- ☐ Feather
- ☐ Fish (2)
- ☐ Flower
- ☐ Frogs (2)
- ☐ Ghost
- ☐ Giraffe
- ☐ Gold coin
- ☐ Heart
- ☐ Hot dog
- ☐ Juggler
- ☐ Mice (2)
- ☐ Nail
- ☐ Paintbrush
- ☐ Piano keys
- ☐ Pig
- ☐ Rabbit
- ☐ Seal
- ☐ Ship
- ☐ Straw hat
- ☐ Telescope
- ☐ Tree
- ☐ Worm

Who is Harold?
Who is going
to shave?

Columbus set sail with his three ships, the Nina, the Pinta, and the Santa Maria, on August 3, 1492.

HUNT FOR COLUMBUS WITH HIS SHIPS AND…

- ☐ Anchor
- ☐ Arrows (2)
- ☐ Barrel of monkeys
- ☐ Basket
- ☐ Bottles (2)
- ☐ Cactus
- ☐ Can
- ☐ Candle
- ☐ Coffeepot
- ☐ Ducky
- ☐ Football
- ☐ Hamburgers (2)
- ☐ Hammer
- ☐ Helmet
- ☐ Horse
- ☐ Lost boot
- ☐ Lunchbox
- ☐ Mermaid
- ☐ Pig
- ☐ Pink fish (3)
- ☐ Pumpkin
- ☐ Rabbit
- ☐ Rat
- ☐ Roller skates
- ☐ Sea serpent
- ☐ Shipwrecked sailor
- ☐ Sock
- ☐ Tires (2)
- ☐ TV set
- ☐ Umbrella
- ☐ Unicorn
- ☐ Worm
- ☐ Would-be surfer

What ship is Columbus on? Which ship is the smallest?

On October 12, 1492 Columbus discovered San Salvador in the Bahamas.

WHERE'S COLUMBUS ON THIS TROPICAL ISLAND IN THE NEW WORLD AND...

☐ Banana peel
☐ Book
☐ Clothespin
☐ Clown
☐ Dog
☐ Duck
☐ Feather
☐ Fish (2)
☐ Flashbulb
☐ Football
☐ Ghost
☐ Ice skates
☐ Kite
☐ Lizard
☐ Lost mitten
☐ Mice (2)
☐ Oars (6)
☐ Painted egg
☐ Parrot
☐ Pencil
☐ Pig
☐ Pottery
☐ Rabbit
☐ Scarecrow
☐ Seesaw
☐ Ships (4)
☐ Snail
☐ Spear
☐ Stars (3)
☐ Sword
☐ Train engine
☐ Trunk
☐ Turtle
☐ Wooden leg

Who wants a cracker?
Who is all wet?

Upon Columbus's return, he was made Admiral of the Ocean and Viceroy of the Indies. On September 25, 1493, he commanded 17 ships and about 1,000 men on his second voyage to the New World.

FIND COLUMBUS AS THE SHIPS SET SAIL AND...

- ☐ Arrow
- ☐ Banana peel
- ☐ Baseball bat
- ☐ Birds (2)
- ☐ Broom
- ☐ Camel
- ☐ Candle
- ☐ Cooking pot
- ☐ Dog
- ☐ Feather
- ☐ Fish (3)
- ☐ Flowerpot
- ☐ Flying bat
- ☐ Fork
- ☐ Ghost
- ☐ Hammer
- ☐ Heart
- ☐ Key
- ☐ Man in a barrel
- ☐ Mouse
- ☐ Pen
- ☐ Quarter moon
- ☐ Question mark
- ☐ Seal
- ☐ Snowman
- ☐ Spoon
- ☐ Star
- ☐ Tent
- ☐ Toothbrush
- ☐ Turtle
- ☐ TV antenna
- ☐ Upside-down tree

How many ships left this time? Who didn't escape from the zoo?